DOGGER

SHIRLEY HUGHES

Lothrop, Lee & Shepard Books
New York

Some other picture books by
Shirley Hughes

Alfie Gets in First
Alfie Gives a Hand
Alfie's Feet
An Evening at Alfie's
Moving Molly
Up and Up
Bathwater's Hot
Noisy
When We Went to the Park
All Shapes and Sizes
Colors
Two Shoes, New Shoes
Out and About
The Big Alfie and Annie Rose Story Book

For Judy and Margaret

First Edition 1 2 3 4 5 6 7 8 9 10

Library of Congress Cataloging in Publication Data
Hughes, Shirley. Dogger / Shirley Hughes.
p. cm. Summary: A youngster is upset by the loss
of his favorite stuffed dog. ISBN 0-688-07980-6
ISBN 0-688-07981-4 (lib. bdg.)
[1. Toys—Fiction.] I. Title. PZ7.H87395Do 1988 [E]—dc19
87-33787 CIP AC.

Once there was a soft brown toy called Dogger.
One of his ears pointed upwards and the other
flopped over. His fur was worn in places because
he was quite old. He belonged to Dave.

Dave was *very* fond
of Dogger. He took him
everywhere.

Sometimes he gave him rides in a wagon.

Sometimes he pulled
him along on a leash
made of string like
a real dog.

When it was cold
he wrapped him
up in a bit of blanket.

Now and again Dave's
Mom said that Dogger was
getting much too dirty. She showed Dave how to
wash him in a bowl of soapy water. Then they
hung him up by his tail on the clothesline to dry.

Dave's baby brother, Joe, liked hard toys. He liked putting them in his mouth and biting on them, because he was getting teeth.

Dave's big sister, Bella, took seven teddies to bed
with her every night. She had to sleep right up
against the wall to stop herself from falling out.
But Dave liked only Dogger.

One afternoon Dave and Mom set out to collect
Bella from school. Mom took Joe in the stroller
and Dave took Dogger. Next to the school gate
where the moms waited was a playground. Some
men with ladders were putting up colored flags.
Mom said that there was going to be a Summer
Fair to get money to buy things for the school.
Dave pushed Dogger up against the railings to
show him what was going on.

Just then the children started to come out of
school. An ice-cream van came around the corner
playing a tune. Bella ran up with her satchel flying.

"Mom, can we have an ice cream?"

Mom gave her the money for two cones. Joe
didn't have a whole ice cream to himself because
he was too dribbly.

On the way home Dave walked beside
the stroller giving Joe licks off his
ice cream. Joe kicked his feet about and
shouted for more in between licks.

At supper Dave was rather quiet.
In the bath he was even quieter.
At bedtime he said,
"I want Dogger."
But Dogger was nowhere to be found.

Mom looked under the bed.

She looked behind
the cupboard.

She searched in the kitchen—

and underneath the stairs.
Dave watched anxiously through
the banisters. Joe watched
through the bars of his crib.

Bella joined in to look for Dogger. She turned out her own toy box in case he was in there, but he wasn't.

When Dad came home he looked for Dogger too. He searched in the shed and down the garden path with a flashlight.

But Dogger was quite lost.

Dave was very sad when he went to bed. Bella kindly lent him one of her teddies to go to sleep with, but it was not the same thing as Dogger. Dave kept waking up in the night and missing him.

The next day was Saturday and they all went to the School Summer Fair. The playground was full of stands and sideshows.

There was a Fancy Dress Parade.

Then there were games, with an Egg-and-Spoon Race

a Wheelbarrow Race

and a Fathers' Race.

Bella was very good at races.
She won the Three-Legged Race
with her friend Barbara.
   "Wouldn't you like to go in
for a race?" they asked Dave.
But Dave didn't feel like racing.
He was missing Dogger
too much.

Then another very exciting thing happened to
Bella. She won first prize in a raffle! It was a huge
yellow teddy bear, wearing a beautiful blue silk
bow. He was almost as big as Dave.

Dave didn't like that teddy at all. At that
moment he didn't like Bella much either because
she kept on winning things. He went off on his
own to look at the stands.

One lady had a toy stand, full of knitted ducks
and cars and baby dolls in bonnets. And there,
at the very back, behind a lot of
other toys, was—

DOGGER!

He was wearing a ticket saying "50¢."

There were a lot of people around the stand. Dave tried to explain to the lady that it was his Dogger, who had got lost and somehow been put on the stand by mistake, but she wasn't listening. He looked in his pocket. He had 10¢ but that wasn't enough. He ran to find Mom and Dad to ask them to buy Dogger back *at once*.

Dave went everywhere in the crowd but he couldn't see Mom and Dad. He thought he was going to cry. At last he found Bella by the cakes. When she heard about Dogger, she and Dave ran back to the toy stand as fast as they could.

But something terrible
had happened. Dogger had
just been bought by
a little girl!

She was already walking
off with him. Dave began to cry.

Bella ran after her and
tried to explain that
Dogger really belonged
to Dave, and could they
please buy him back?

But the little girl said,
"No."

She said that she had
bought Dogger with her
own money and she
wanted him. She held
on to him very tightly.

Dave cried and cried.

And the little girl started to cry too.

But out of the corner of her eye she caught sight of Bella's big yellow teddy. She stopped crying and put out her hand to stroke his beautiful blue silk bow.

Then Bella did something *very* kind.

"Would you swap this teddy for my brother's dog?" she asked. Right away the little girl stopped crying and began to smile. She held out Dogger to Dave, took the big teddy instead, and went off with him in her arms.

Then Dave smiled too.

He hugged Dogger and he hugged Bella around the waist.

"Thank you, Bella," he said.

That night Dave had Dogger in bed beside him.

Bella was practicing somersaults.

"Will you miss that big teddy?" Dave asked her.

"No," said Bella. "I didn't like him much really.
He was too big and his eyes were too staring.
Anyway, if I had another teddy in my bed there
wouldn't be room for me."